For Stacey Barney, with gratitude for 5,199
(and counting!) days of kindness —I.L.

For my baby boy coming 2022 —J.P.

G. P. Putnam's Sons
An imprint of Penguin Random House LLC, New York

First published in the United States of America by G. P. Putnam's Sons,
an imprint of Penguin Random House LLC, 2022

Text copyright © 2022 by Irene Latham | Illustrations copyright © 2022 by Junghwa Park

Penguin supports copyright. Copyright fuels creativity, encourages diverse voices, promotes
free speech, and creates a vibrant culture. Thank you for buying an authorized edition of this book
and for complying with copyright laws by not reproducing, scanning, or distributing any part of it in
any form without permission. You are supporting writers and allowing Penguin to continue to publish books
for every reader. | G. P. Putnam's Sons is a registered trademark of Penguin Random House LLC. | Visit us
online at penguinrandomhouse.com | Library of Congress Cataloging-in-Publication Data | Names: Latham,
Irene, author. | Park, Junghwa, illustrator. | Title: 12 days of kindness / written by Irene Latham; illustrated
by Junghwa Park. | Other titles: Twelve days of kindness | Twelve days of Christmas (English folk song) |
Description: New York: G. P. Putnam's Sons, 2022. | Summary: In this variation on the song "The Twelve Days
of Christmas," a child explores the many ways to be kind. | Identifiers: LCCN 2021044865 (print) |
LCCN 2021044866 (ebook) | ISBN 9780525514169 (hardcover) | ISBN 9780525514190 (kindle edition) |
ISBN 9780525514176 (epub) | Subjects: LCSH: Children's songs—United States—Texts. | CYAC: Kindness—Songs
and music. | Songs. | LCGFT: Picture books. | Song texts. | Classification: LCC PZ8.3.L3443 Aah 2022 (print) |
LCC PZ8.3.L3443 (ebook) | DDC 782.42 [E]—dc23/eng/20211027 | LC record available at
https://lccn.loc.gov/2021044865 | LC ebook record available at https://lccn.loc.gov/2021044866 |
Manufactured in China | ISBN 9780525514169 | 10 9 8 7 6 5 4 3 2 1 | TOPL

Design by Eileen Savage | Text set in Filson Pro | The art was done in watercolor, colored pencil, oil pastel,
and gouache on watercolor paper and colored paper. It was edited in Adobe Photoshop. | The publisher
does not have any control over and does not assume any responsibility for author or third-party
websites or their content.

12 DAYS of KINDNESS

written by

IRENE LATHAM

illustrated by

JUNGHWA PARK

putnam

G. P. Putnam's Sons

On the first day of kindness, I will give to you a hug that's warm and true.

 On the second day of kindness, I will give to you two open doors . . .

and a hug that's warm and true.

On the third day of kindness, I will give to you three wide smiles . . .

two open doors
and a hug that's warm and true.

4 On the fourth day of kindness, I will give to you four fresh pencils . . .

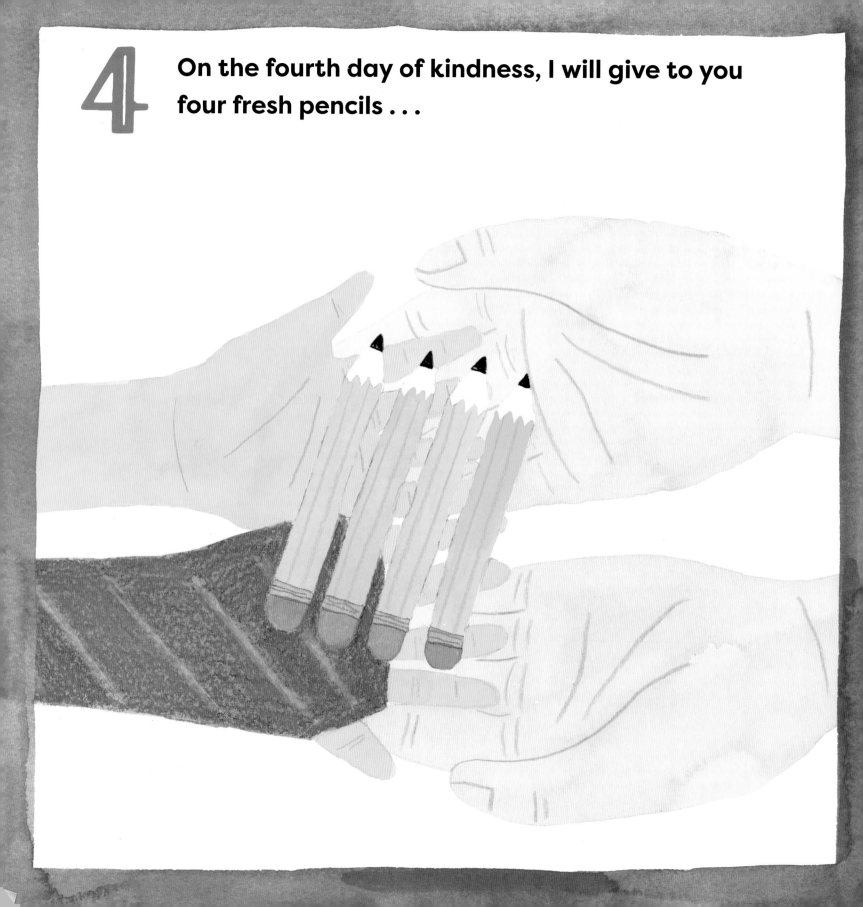

three wide smiles
two open doors
and a hug that's warm and true.

On the fifth day of kindness, I will give to you five thank-you notes . . .

four fresh pencils
three wide smiles
two open doors
and a hug that's warm and true.

6

On the sixth day of kindness, I will give to you six salutations . . .

five thank-you notes
four fresh pencils
three wide smiles
two open doors
and a hug that's warm and true.

7 On the seventh day of kindness, I will give to you seven shared snacks . . .

six salutations
five thank-you notes
four fresh pencils
three wide smiles
two open doors
and a hug that's warm and true.

8

On the eighth day of kindness, I will give to you eight encouraging words . . .

seven shared snacks
six salutations
five thank-you notes
four fresh pencils
three wide smiles
two open doors
and a hug that's warm and true.

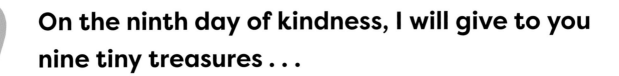

On the ninth day of kindness, I will give to you nine tiny treasures . . .

eight encouraging words

seven shared snacks

six salutations

five thank-you notes

four fresh pencils

three wide smiles

two open doors

and a hug that's warm and true.

On the tenth day of kindness, I will give to you ten minutes listening . . .

nine tiny treasures
eight encouraging words
seven shared snacks
six salutations
five thank-you notes
four fresh pencils
three wide smiles
two open doors
and a hug that's warm and true.

11 On the eleventh day of kindness, I will give to you eleven hands a-helping . . .

ten minutes listening
nine tiny treasures
eight encouraging words
seven shared snacks
six salutations
five thank-you notes
four fresh pencils
three wide smiles
two open doors
and a hug that's
warm and true.

On the twelfth day of kindness, I will give to you twelve good-night kisses . . .

eleven hands a-helping
ten minutes listening
nine tiny treasures
eight encouraging words
seven shared snacks
six salutations
five thank-you notes
four fresh pencils
three wide smiles
two open doors
and a hug that's
warm and true.